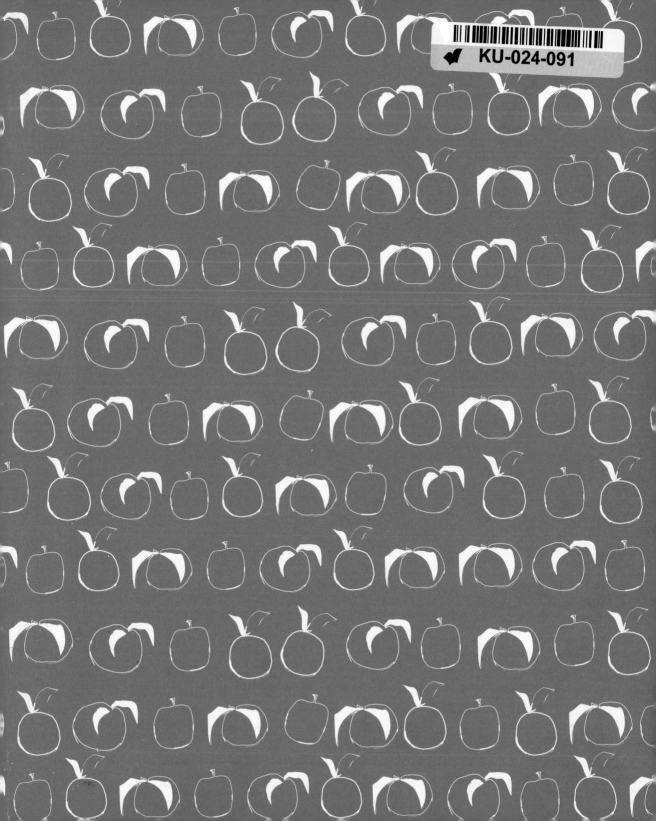

Apple Pigs

To Livia Jack
with love from Bubba

Apple Pigs

Ruth Gary Orbach

 National Trust

Once in our garden
there stood an old tree –
no blossoms, no leaves,
no fruit for me.

Some people said
"Chop it down, chop it down.
Sell it for firewood
up in the town."

But the tree had a
secret that only I shared
It whispered to me
that nobody cared.

"I care," I said.
"And I'll do my best."
"All right," said the tree.
"Then I'll do the rest."

So I cleared away rubbish,
I raked and I hoed,
I planted some flowers,
and kept the grass mowed.

When the Spring came,
bringing warm sun and rain,
my tree stood tall
and proud again.

The branches grew leaves
as never before,
but that wasn't all –
there was still to be more.

Branches, leaves, blossoms,
and apples at last.
At first they were small,
but they grew very fast.

Plenty of apples,
delicious to eat,
juicy and crunchy,
crisp and sweet.

The more we ate
the more they grew.
We began to wonder
what to do.

We ate apples for breakfast,
sliced on toast.

We ate apples on Sunday,
baked with the roast.

Apples for dinner,
apples for tea –
too many apples,
we all agreed.

We just couldn't eat them.
"Too many," we said.
So we stored them
under the biggest bed.

We packed them in baskets,
in boxes, in trunks.
We stuffed them in cupboards
and up in the bunks.

The bathtub was full,
the basin piled high,
they hung from the ceiling –
like clouds in the sky.

The more we ate,
the more they grew,
the more we wondered
what to do.

Apples were lying
all over the ground –
more baskets and boxes
just could not be found.

We wrapped them in blankets,
we wrapped them in rugs,
we piled them in wagons
and bowls and jugs.

They fell from the ceiling
and rolled round the floor,
but still my tree
grew more and more.

APPLE FEAST
come man
come bird
come woolly beast

The more we ate
the more they grew.
At last I knew
what we must do.

The sign we hung
said "Apple Feast!
Come man, come bird,
Come woolly beast."

And come they did,
from far and wide.
Some simply could
not fit inside.

Women and men,
girls and boys,
hippo and yak –
what a noise!

We sang and danced,
then sang some more,
and then ate apples
by the score.

Apple fritters,
apple-ade,
apple custard
Father made.

Apple strudel,
apples dried,
apple pigs were
Mother's pride.

As for me,
I love to bake.
I started off
with apple cake.

Then toffee-apples,
hung up high,
apple pan dowdy,
and Dutch apple pie.

Some ate cores,
some ate peelings,
some ate apples
from the ceiling.

Soon the apples
were no more.
We'd gobbled up our
whole great store.

At last we heard,
"Goodbye, Goodnight!
We'll come again,
if that's all right."

So now each year
we have a feast,
for man and bird
and woolly beast.

I hope next year
at Summer's end
you'll come along
and bring a friend.

First published in the United Kingdom in 2015 by
National Trust Books
1 Gower Street
London WC1E 6HD

An imprint of Pavilion Books Group

ISBN: 9781843653028

A CIP catalogue record for this book is available from the British Library.

10 9 8 7 6 5 4 3 2 1

Reproduction by Mission Productions, Hong Kong
Printed and bound by 1010 Printing International Ltd, China

This book can be ordered direct from the publisher
at the website: www.pavilionbooks.com, or try your local bookshop.
Also available at National Trust shops or www.shop.nationaltrust.org.uk.